BIG
AND
LITTLE

BY
WILLIAM JAY SMITH

ILLUSTRATED BY
DON BOLOGNESE

WORDSONG

Published by Wordsong
Boyds Mills Press, Inc.
A Highlights Company
910 Church Street
Honesdale, Pennsylvania 18431

Publisher Cataloging-in-Publication Data

Smith, William Jay, 1918 – .
Big and little / by William Jay Smith ; illustrated by
Don Bolognese.
[32] p. : col. ill. ; cm.
Summary: Light verses about large and small.
ISBN 1-56397-023-6
1. Children's poetry — American. [1. American poetry.   2. Humorous
poetry.]   I. Bolognese, Don, ill.   II. Title.
811 / .54 — dc20   [E]   1992
Library of Congress Catalog Card Number: 91-66057

Distributed by St. Martin's Press

Cover and interior design by M 'N O Production Services, Inc.

Printed in Hong Kong

For Marissa
and
Alexandre

There once was a man
With a little head
And very big feet
Who laughed and said:

"Jig-jig-jig—
Spin and whirl—
Hello, little boy!
Hello, little girl!

Little and big,
Big and little!
A little teapot,
A big teakettle.

Big and little,
　　Little and big—

　　A big fat hog,
　　　　A pink little pig.

　　　　Jig-jig-jig—spin and whirl—
　　　　　　Hello, little boy! Hello, little girl!"

　　　　　　So he danced a jig,
　　　　　　　　Though his feet were big,
　　　　　　　　　　And when he finished,
　　　　　　　　　　　　He laughed and said:

"Would you like to hear—
It may sound queer—
About a boy who grew so tall
He outgrew house and home and all?

Great big gawky Gumbo Cole
Couldn't stop growing to save his soul.

Gave up eating, gave up drink,
Sat in a closet, hoped to shrink.

But he grew and grew
Till he burst the door,

His head went through
To the upper floor,

His feet reached down
To the cellar door.

He grew still more
Till the house came down,

And Gumbo Cole
Stepped out on the town
And smashed it in
Like an old anthill!

Never stopped growing,
        Never will.

Ten times as tall as a telephone pole,
Too big for his breeches, Gumbo Cole!"

And then the man with the little head
And the very big feet bowed and said:

"Big and little,
Little and big—
Fling your leg
And fling your arm—
A big green snake,
A little pink worm,

A big umbrella,
A little fan—
Spin and whirl,"
Said the man.

"Whirl and spin—
Jig-jig-jig—
Spin and whirl—
Good-bye, little boy!
Good-bye, little girl!"

If you want to read
About people big and small,
Things that are tiny,
Things that are tall,
Then have a look
At the very next page
Of this little book.

There once was a man
With a middle-sized head
And middle-sized feet
By a little house
In a little street.

He had a tall hat.
He had a small cane,
And he laughed and said
Again and again:

"How big is big?
How high is high?
How small is an acorn?
How tall is the sky?

Big and little,
  Little and big!
    All things—all
      Are big and small.

There are big oak trees,
Little pieces of cheese,
Big bluebottle flies,
Little blue eyes,
Big gorillas,
Little umbrellas.

A big full moon,
A little teaspoon.
Big brown kangaroos,
Little red shoes.

A big brass band,

A grain of sand.

A big octopus,
A little platypus.

Big trees,
    little branches,
Little grapes,
    big bunches.

Big horses
　　　that prance,
Little girls
　　　who dance.

Big boxes that hide
Other boxes inside.

Boxes in boxes,
More! What fun!
And inside this one—
Inside that—
A little hat!   And in the hat—

A little surprise—
A bird that flies!

All things—all
Are big and small!
And you may see
Them—one and all—
When you close your eyes.

Big and little,
    Little and big!
        Spin and whirl
            And dance a jig.

Big apples, big peaches,
Big waves, big beaches.
Little holes, little huts,
Little shells, little nuts.

Jig-jig-jig—
Spin and whirl—
Goodnight, little boy!
Goodnight, little girl!"

And they watched the man
With the middle-sized head
And the middle-sized feet,
As he danced away
Down the little street.

"Little boy, little girl,
Sweet dreams!" he said.
Then they closed the book
And went to bed.